This book belongs to

....

....

This edition first published in 2010 by Alligator Books Ltd.
Cupcake is an imprint of Alligator Books Ltd
Gadd House, Arcadia Avenue, London N3 2JU

Written by Katherine Sully
Illustrated by Sam Chaffey

Printed in China 0042

PIG'S EGG

cupcake

Pig loved the farmyard. There was always something going on. Pig loved being a pig too. But sometimes he couldn't help feeling left out.

Goose could fly.

Duck could fly.

Even Hen could fly.

But try as he might, Pig just couldn't seem to get the hang of it.

Then, one spring morning, Pig went to see Hen.

"What are you doing?" he asked Hen.
"I'm hatching an egg," said Hen.

Just then, the egg cracked and out popped...

...a fluffy chick.

"You'll have to excuse me, Pig," said Hen.
"I'm far too busy to talk to you now."

Pig went to see Duck.

"What are you doing?" he asked Duck.
"I'm hatching an egg," said Duck.

Just then, the egg cracked and out popped...

...a fluffy duckling.

"You'll have to excuse me, Pig," said Duck.
"I'm far too busy to talk to you now."

Pig went to see Goose.

"What are you doing?" he asked Goose.
"I'm hatching an egg," said Goose.

Just then, the egg cracked and out popped...

...a fluffy gosling.

"You'll have to excuse me, Pig," said Goose.
"I'm far too busy to talk to you now."

Pig went back to his sty feeling even more left out. Pig was just tucking into his dinner when he spotted something on the ground.

It was shaped like an egg.
"I've laid an egg!" cried Pig.
He didn't feel left out any more.

Pig looked after his egg carefully.
Hen brought her chick to visit Pig.

"What's that you've got there, Pig?"
asked Hen.
"It's my egg!" said Pig, proudly.

"Pigs don't lay eggs," said Hen. "It looks
like a turnip."
"It's not a turnip," said Pig. "It's an egg."

Duck brought her duckling to visit Pig.

"What's that you've got there, Pig?"
asked Duck.
"It's my egg," said Pig.
"That's not an egg," said Duck. "It's a turnip."

"It's not a turnip," said
Pig. "It's an egg!"

Goose brought her gosling to visit Pig.

"What's that you've got there, Pig?" asked Goose.

"IT'S NOT A TURNIP," said Pig. "IT'S AN EGG!"

But when the egg didn't crack, Pig began to wonder.

"Maybe they're right," thought Pig, sadly. "Maybe it is a turnip." Pig sighed. "There's only one way to find out — I'll eat it."

Pig opened his mouth wide but just as he was about to bite into it, he noticed a tiny hole.

The tiny hole
got bigger.

And bigger.

And something very
small wriggled out of it.

"My baby!" cried Pig with pride.

Pig took great care of his baby.
He fed it cabbage leaves and
it got fatter and fatter.

Pig called to Hen and Duck and Goose.

"Come and see my baby," he said.

But when they reached the sty, there was no sign of Pig's baby. Instead there was a crinkly, green egg.

Hen and Duck and Goose patted Pig.

"Never mind..." they said.

The next morning, something VERY strange happened. As Pig lay sighing and staring at the crinkly, green egg, it began to crack. Out wriggled the most beautiful creature Pig had ever seen.

It flapped its wings and flew away.
Pig jumped up and danced after it.

"What are you doing, Pig?" asked Hen,
Duck and Goose.

"You'll have to excuse me," said Pig.
"I'm far too busy to talk to you now.
I'm teaching my baby to fly!"